Snap!

The little turtle

can see the grass.

The little turtle
can see the trees.

The little turtle
can see the flowers.

The little turtle

can see the water.

The little turtle
can see a duck.

11

The little turtle
can see the frog.

The little turtle
can see a fly.

Snap!